STONE ARCH BOOKS
a capstone imprint

STONE ARCH BOOKS™
Published in 2013
A Capstone Imprint
1710 Roe Crest Drive
North Mankato, MN 56003
www.capstonepub.com

DC Comics
1700 Broadway, New York, NY 10019
A Warner Bros. Entertainment Company

Originally published by DC Comics in the U.S. in single magazine form as Batman: The Brave and the Bold #7.

Cataloging-in-Publication Data is available at the Library of Congress website:
ISBN: 978-1-4342-4707-0 (library binding)

Summary: Here comes the Doom Patrol! And they want Batman to help them out with...General Immortus? But we just shipped him off last issue!

STONE ARCH BOOKS
Ashley C. Andersen Zantop *Publisher*
Michael Dahl *Editorial Director*
Donald Lemke & Sean Tulien *Editors*
Heather Kindseth *Creative Director*
Hilary Wacholz *Designer*
Kathy McColley *Production Specialist*

DC COMICS
Rachel Gluckstern & Michael Siglain *Original U.S. Editors*
Harvey Richards *U.S. Assistant Editor*

Printed in China by Nordica.
1012/CA21201277
092012 006935NORDS13

BATMAN
THE BRAVE AND THE BOLD
THE SECRET OF THE DOOMSDAY DESIGN!
J. TORRES.....WRITER
J. BONE.....PENCILLER
J. BONE.....INKER
HEROIC AGE.....COLORIST
TRAVIS LANHAM.....LETTERER
SCOTT JERALDS.....COVER ARTIST

YOU HAVE NOT SEEN THE LAST OF ME, BATMAN!
CIRCE'S GETTING AWAY--
--BUT SHE IS LEAVING BEHIND HER PETS TO KEEP US COMPANY! HOW GENEROUS!
HIS NAME IS THE OLYMPIAN.
HERE, KITTY, KITTIES!
HE IS THE FOUNDING MEMBER OF THE GLOBAL GUARDIANS.
WHAM
"THE SUPERMAN OF GREECE."

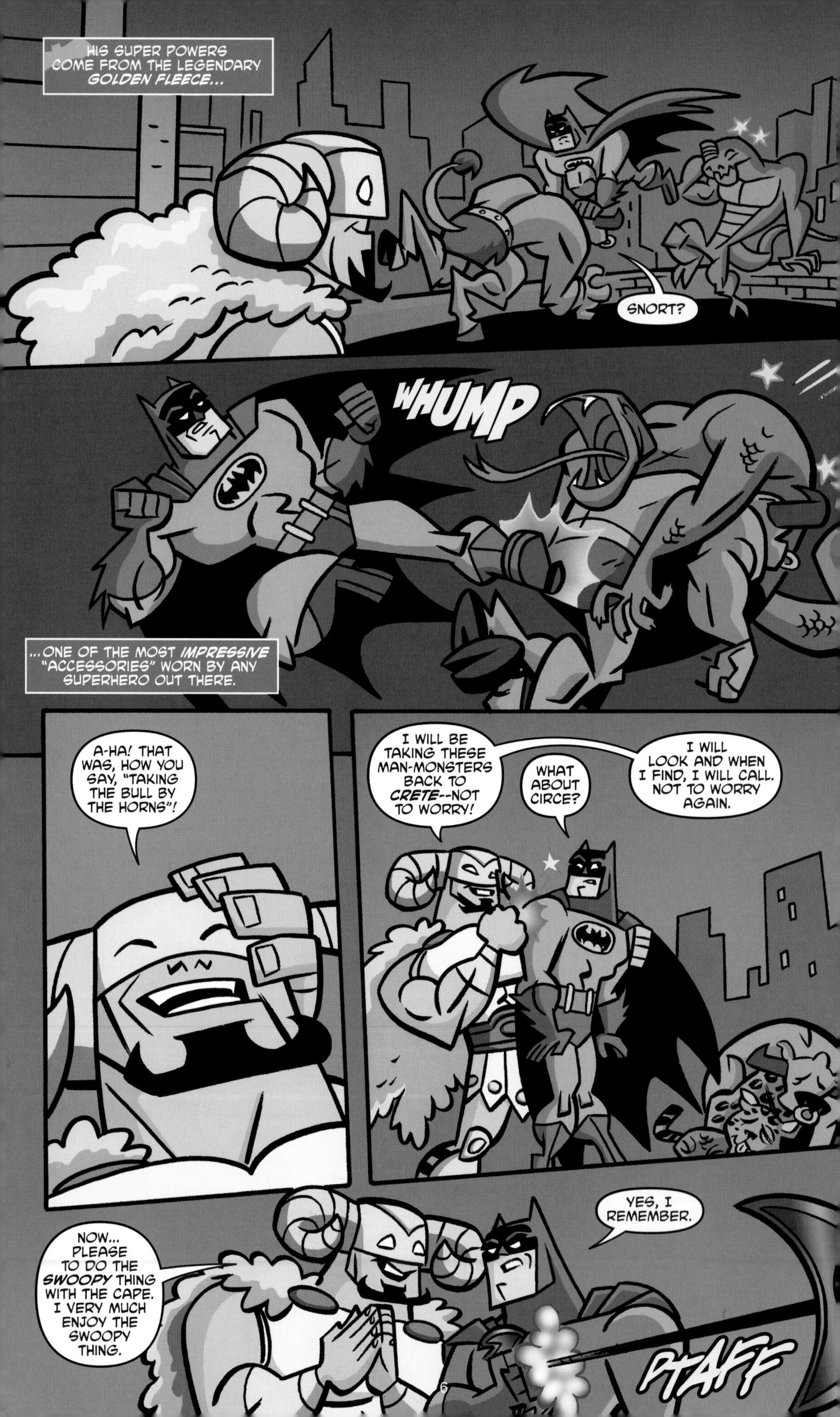
HIS SUPER POWERS COME FROM THE LEGENDARY *GOLDEN FLEECE*...
SNORT?
WHUMP
...ONE OF THE MOST *IMPRESSIVE* "ACCESSORIES" WORN BY ANY SUPERHERO OUT THERE.
A-HA! THAT WAS, HOW YOU SAY, "TAKING THE BULL BY THE HORNS"!
I WILL BE TAKING THESE MAN-MONSTERS BACK TO *CRETE*--NOT TO WORRY!
WHAT ABOUT CIRCE?
I WILL LOOK AND WHEN I FIND, I WILL CALL. NOT TO WORRY AGAIN.
NOW... PLEASE TO DO THE *SWOOPY* THING WITH THE CAPE. I VERY MUCH ENJOY THE SWOOPY THING.
YES, I REMEMBER.
PTAFF

HA-HA-HA! I *LOVE* IT!
SWOOOP

MAYBE I SHOULD CONSULT DR. FATE OR ZATANNA ABOUT COMBATING SORCERY...
...TO BE READY THE NEXT TIME CIRCE TURNS UP.
BATMAN! THIS IS DR. CAULDER!
DR. NILES "THE CHIEF" CAULDER...
...LEADER OF THE DOOM PATROL, THE WORLD'S STRANGEST HEROES!
THE DOOM PATROL NEEDS YOUR HELP!
ROBOTMAN, ELASTI-GIRL, AND NEGATIVE MAN HAVE BEEN TAKEN CAPTIVE.
I SUSPECT *GENERAL IMMORTUS* IS BEHIND THIS. YOU KNOW HOW HE ENJOYS ATTACKING MY TEAM.
SAY NO MORE, DOC. JUST TELL ME WHERE THEY ARE.
JUST LOOK UP, BATMAN...
DADDY! DADDY! I'VE BEEN LOOKING ALL OVER FOR YOU!

BEAST BOY MANAGED TO TRACK DOWN THEIR LOCATION, BUT I DIDN'T THINK HE SHOULD ATTEMPT A RESCUE ON HIS OWN.
"DADDY"-- GET IT, BATMAN?
NO TIME FOR JOKES. GET IN THE CAR AND DON'T FORGET TO PUT YOUR SEATBELT ON.
YES, SIR.
VRRROOOM

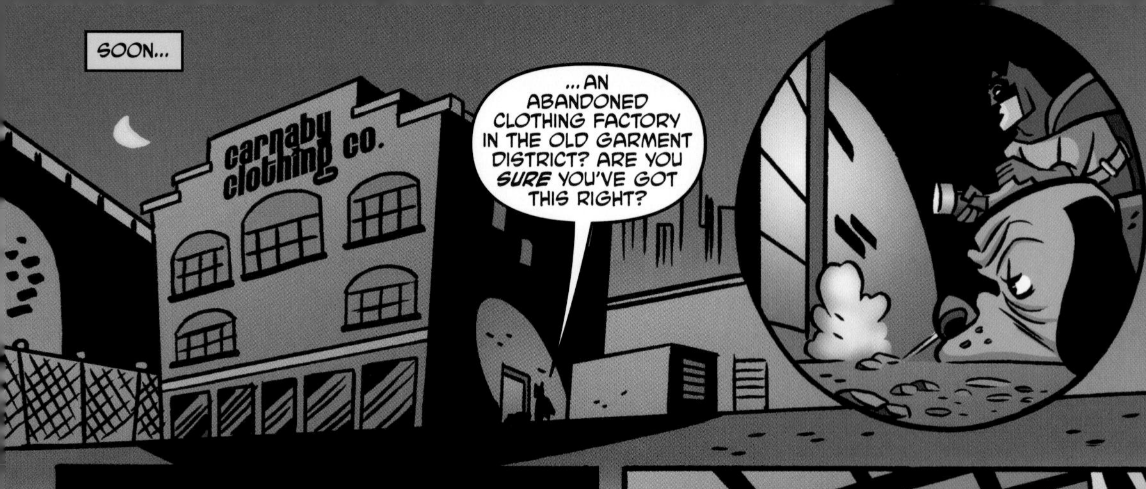
SOON...
carnaby clothing co.
...AN ABANDONED CLOTHING FACTORY IN THE OLD GARMENT DISTRICT? ARE YOU *SURE* YOU'VE GOT THIS RIGHT?

YEAH, BATMAN! I TRACKED *ELASTI-GIRL'S* SCENT TO THIS PLACE!

UH... BATMAN? I THINK THAT *MANNEQUIN* OVER THERE JUST... MOVED?

THEY'RE *ALL* ON THE MOVE!

BOFF
BAMMM

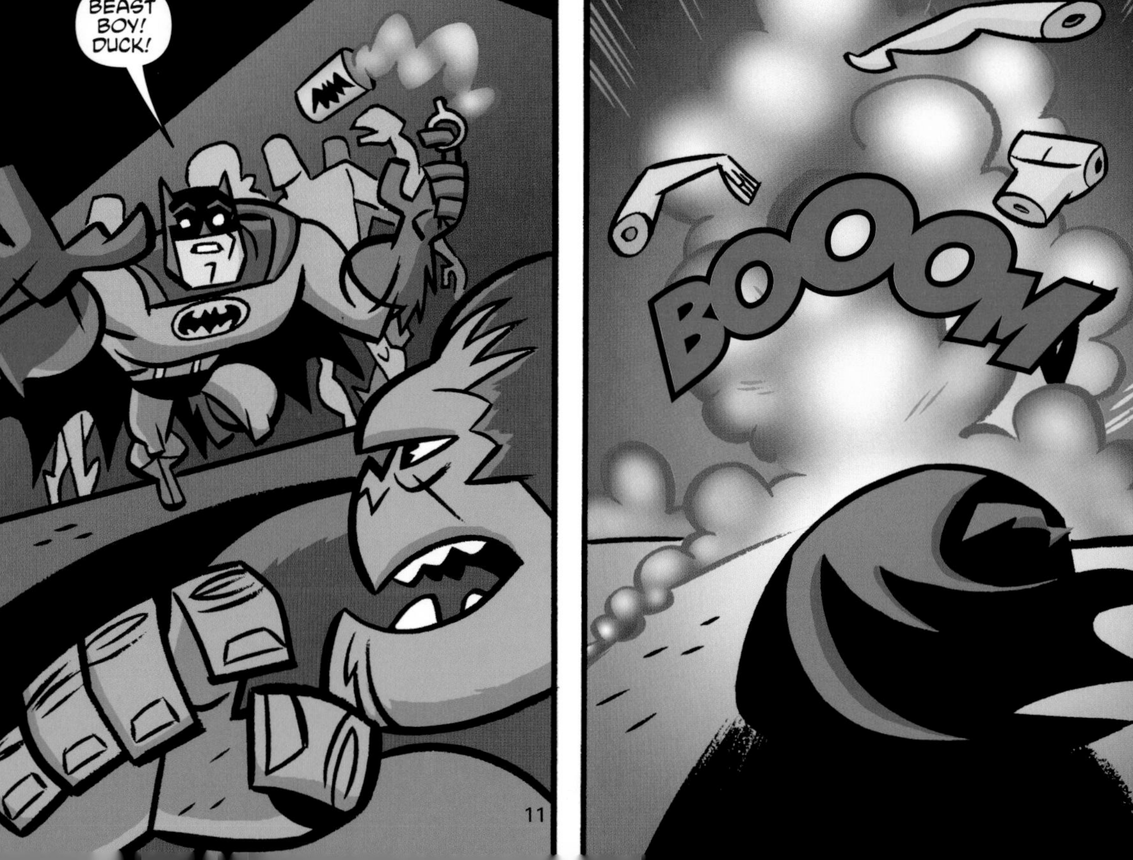
BEAST BOY! DUCK!
BOOOM

SHHK
SHHK
CUT IT OUT. THAT'S NOT FUNNY.
HELLO? WHOEVER'S OUT THERE--
--HELP! I'M DOWN HERE!
THAT'S ROBOTMAN'S VOICE!

DON'T WORRY, DUDE! BEAST BOY IS HERE TO SAVE YOU! AND I BROUGHT BAT--

--MAN. OH, MAN... WHAT HAPPENED TO YOU? THE REST OF YOU!
I DON'T KNOW... I WOKE UP LIKE THIS... I DON'T EVEN REMEMBER HOW I GOT HERE...

LOOKS LIKE SOMEONE'S BEEN... EXAMINING YOU.
GENERAL IMMORTUS HAS BEEN DYING TO TEAR APART THE DOOM PATROL!
YES, BUT... THIS FACTORY, THE MANNEQUIN "GUARDS," THIS ROOM... DOESN'T LOOK LIKE THE WORK OF IMMORTUS.
WAIT! OVER THERE...

IT'S NEGATIVE MAN!
HEY, KID. GLAD TO SEE YOU. BUT YOU NEED TO KEEP YOUR DISTANCE...
...SOMEONE TOOK MY LEAD-LINED BANDAGES, SO YOU DON'T WANT TO GET TOO CLOSE TO MY *RADIOACTIVE* BODY!
HERE, SHRED THIS LAB COAT TO MAKE NEW BANDAGES AND THEN *SPRAY* IT WITH THIS STUFF.
WHAT IS THAT?

LIQUID *LEAD.*
I USE IT TO KEEP SUPERMAN'S X-RAY EYES OUT OF MY DIARY.
YOU KEEP A DIARY?
RIIIP

OH, NOW *YOU'RE* JUST TRYING TO BE FUNNY...
GOTCHA.

MAY I?

BY ALL MEANS.

SHORTLY...
THIS WAY! I'VE FOUND...
ELASTI-GIRL!
BABY BOY! I'M SO HAPPY TO SEE YOU... BUT MIND BACKING UP A BIT?
LET ME GUESS, SOMEONE STOLE *YOUR* CLOTHES, TOO?
WHAT DO YOU PEOPLE THINK YOU'RE DOING--
FFFT
--HEEEEERE?

AFTER ANOTHER QUICK CHANGE...
A LITTLE BIG, BUT IT'LL DO! NOW, LET'S GO GET GENERAL IMMORTUS!
BUT GENERAL IMMORTUS *ISN'T* BEHIND THIS.
YOU KEEP SAYING THAT, BATS! WHAT ARE YOU GETTING AT?
IMMORTUS WOULD ATTACK WITH ROBOT *SOLDIERS,* BUT NOT MECHANICAL *MANNEQUINS.*

HE'D TAKE YOU APART, ROBOTMAN, FOR *GOOD.* NOT JUST STEAL YOUR ARMORED BODY.
OR OUR CLOTHES.

AND THIS IS THE *CARNABY* FACTORY, NAMED AFTER A STREET IN LONDON KNOWN FOR ITS CLOTHING STORES AND AS THE BIRTHPLACE OF "MOD" FASHION.
WAIT, ARE YOU SAYING WE WERE KIDNAPPED BY...

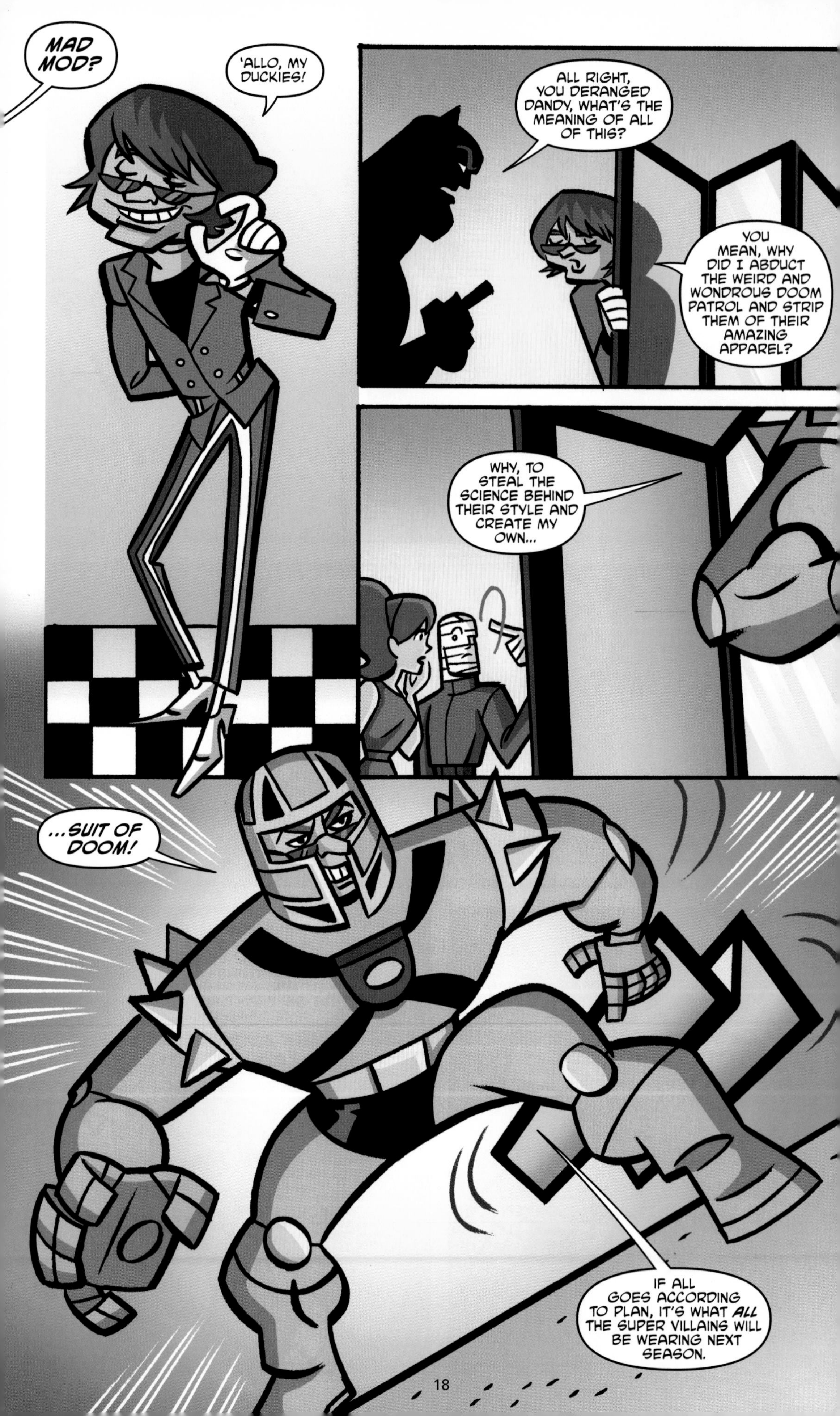
MAD MOD?
'ALLO, MY DUCKIES!
ALL RIGHT, YOU DERANGED DANDY, WHAT'S THE MEANING OF ALL OF THIS?
YOU MEAN, WHY DID I ABDUCT THE WEIRD AND WONDROUS DOOM PATROL AND STRIP THEM OF THEIR AMAZING APPAREL?
WHY, TO STEAL THE SCIENCE BEHIND THEIR STYLE AND CREATE MY OWN...
...SUIT OF DOOM!
IF ALL GOES ACCORDING TO PLAN, IT'S WHAT *ALL* THE SUPER VILLAINS WILL BE WEARING NEXT SEASON.

BUT BEFORE I PUBLICLY UNVEIL MY BRILLIANT NEW LINE OF COMBAT ARMOUR, I NEED TO TAKE *THIS* ONE FOR A "TEST RUN."
I USED TO BE A *TEST PILOT*, SO COME FLY WITH ME, YOU KOOK OF A CLOTHESHORSE!
HATE TO BE NEGATIVE, MAN, BUT THIS ARMOUR'S LINING IS MADE FROM YOUR "SPECIALLY TREATED" BANDAGES...
KONK
...SO YOU CAN'T TOUCH ME!
KRAAK

THEN TRY ME ON FOR SIZE!
OH, I HAVE, LOVE. DID I FAIL TO MENTION THAT THIS COMES IN SHORT SLEEVES...
...AS WELL AS LONG THANKS TO THE "STRETCHY" NANO-FIBERS BORROWED FROM YOUR COSTUME?
KRRRUNK
HERE, HANG ON TO HIM.

OH, NO. WE AIN'T SITTING THIS ONE OUT, ARE WE, SPROUT?
TIME FOR A DRESSING DOWN, MADMAN!
BLIMEY!
KZZAAT
WHAT CHEEK!
NGGG!
HEY, MODDY, HAVEN'T YOU HEARD?

GREEN IS THE NEW BLACK!

THAT'S IT, KID! HIT HIM WITH A LEFT! THEN A RIGHT! THEN ANOTHER RIGHT!
WHAP
WOP
WHAP

WHAK
A LITTLE KNOCK-OUT DART SHOULD DO THE TRICK.
FFFT
I HOPE YOU LIKE STRIPES, MAD MOD, BECAUSE THAT'S WHAT YOU'LL BE WEARING IN PRISON.
OHHHH BOTHERRRR...

LATER AT THE DOOM PATROL'S HEADQUARTERS...
THERE YOU GO, ROBOTMAN.
THANKS, CHIEF. I FEEL A WHOLE LOT BETTER NOW.
BOY, AM I GLAD TO BE WEARING THESE CLOTHES AGAIN.
REALLY? I'VE BEEN CONSIDERING A MAKEOVER. HOW DO YOU THINK I'D LOOK IN A TRENCHCOAT?
THANKS AGAIN FOR SAVING OUR HIDES. IN MY CASE, QUITE LITERALLY.
YOU'RE WELCOME, BUT I REALLY SHOULD GET GOING NOW.
WAIT, BATMAN...
...THE ANIMAL-VEGETABLE-MINERAL MAN IS ON THE LOOSE!
THE "ANIMAL-VEGETABLE-MINERAL MAN"? MAYBE I'LL STICK AROUND. THIS COULD BE MY GREATEST ADVENTURE YET...
THE END.

MAD MOD

Mad Mod is a former fashion designer with a fabulous sense of style but not the good sense to use his talents for good instead of evil. He may be the best-dressed super-villain in history, but history also shows he's the worst at getting away with his crimes.

TOP SECRET:

Mad Mod first faced off against the Teen Titans and to this day has his design on their demise.

DOOM PATROL

The Doom Patol are: former racecar driver now the steel sentinel Robotman, former hollywood actress now the size-shifting Elasti-Girl, former test pilot now the Radioactive Man, and former orphan now the shape-shifting Beast Boy, led by Dr. Niles "The Chief" Caulder. The Doom Patrol often battles evil in the form of villains and monsters as strange and weird as they are.

TOP SECRET:

Each member of the team revived their powers after tragic accidents, but they have overcome their tragedy to help others in trouble.

CREATORS

J. TORRES WRITER

J. Torres won the Shuster Award for Outstanding Writer for his work on *Batman: Legends of the Dark Knight*, *Love As a Foreign Language*, and *Teen Titans Go*. He is also the writer of the Eisner Award nominated *Alison Dare* and the YALSA listed *Days Like This* and *Lola: A Ghost Story*. Other comic book credits include *Avatar: The Last Airbender*, *Legion of Super-Heroes in the 31st Century*, *Ninja Scroll*, *Wonder Girl*, *Wonder Woman*, and *WALL-E: Recharge.*

J. BONE ILLUSTRATOR

J.Bone is a Toronto based illustrator and comic book artist. Besides *DC Super Friends*, he has worked on comic books such as *Spiderman: Tangled Web*, *Mr. Gum*, *Gotham Girls*, and *Madman Adventures*. He is also the co-creator of the *Alison Dare* comic book series.

GLOSSARY

abandoned [uh-BAN-duhnd] - empty, or left forever

captive [KAP-tiv] - a person or an animal that has been taken prisoner

deranged [di-RAYNJD] - insane

legendary [LEJ-uhn-dare-ee] - something from a legend, or story handed down from earlier times. Legends are often based on fact, but they are not entirely true.

literally [LIT-ur-uh-lee] - exactly how it is said or written

radioactive [ray-dee-oh-AK-tiv] - giving off harmful radiaton

sorcery [SOR-sur-ee] - the art of using magical spells and incantations

unveil [uhn-VALE] - reveal or disclose

VISUAL QUESTIONS & PROMPTS

1. In the panel below, Batman and Beast Boy are sneaking up to a building. Why do you think the artists included a smaller, circular panel on top of the bottom one? How does it help you understand what's going on in the story?

2. Why do you think Negative Man's speech balloons are different than everyone else's? Why do you think the artists chose to draw them that way?

3. Why do the speech balloons in the panel below have jagged tails? Why do you think the artists chose to draw them that way?

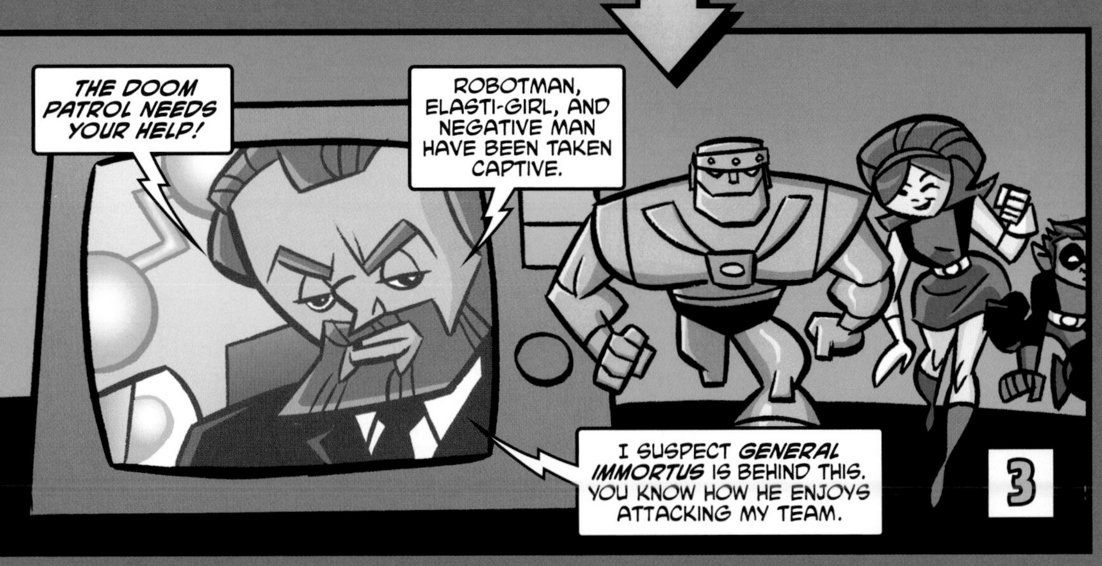

4. Beast Boy can shapeshift into any animal he desires. How does this ability help him solve problems in this comic book? What are some other animal forms that might come in handy for fighting crime?

READ THEM ALL!

THE
FUN DOESN'T
STOP HERE!
DISCOVER MORE AT....
WWW.CAPSTONEKIDS.COM

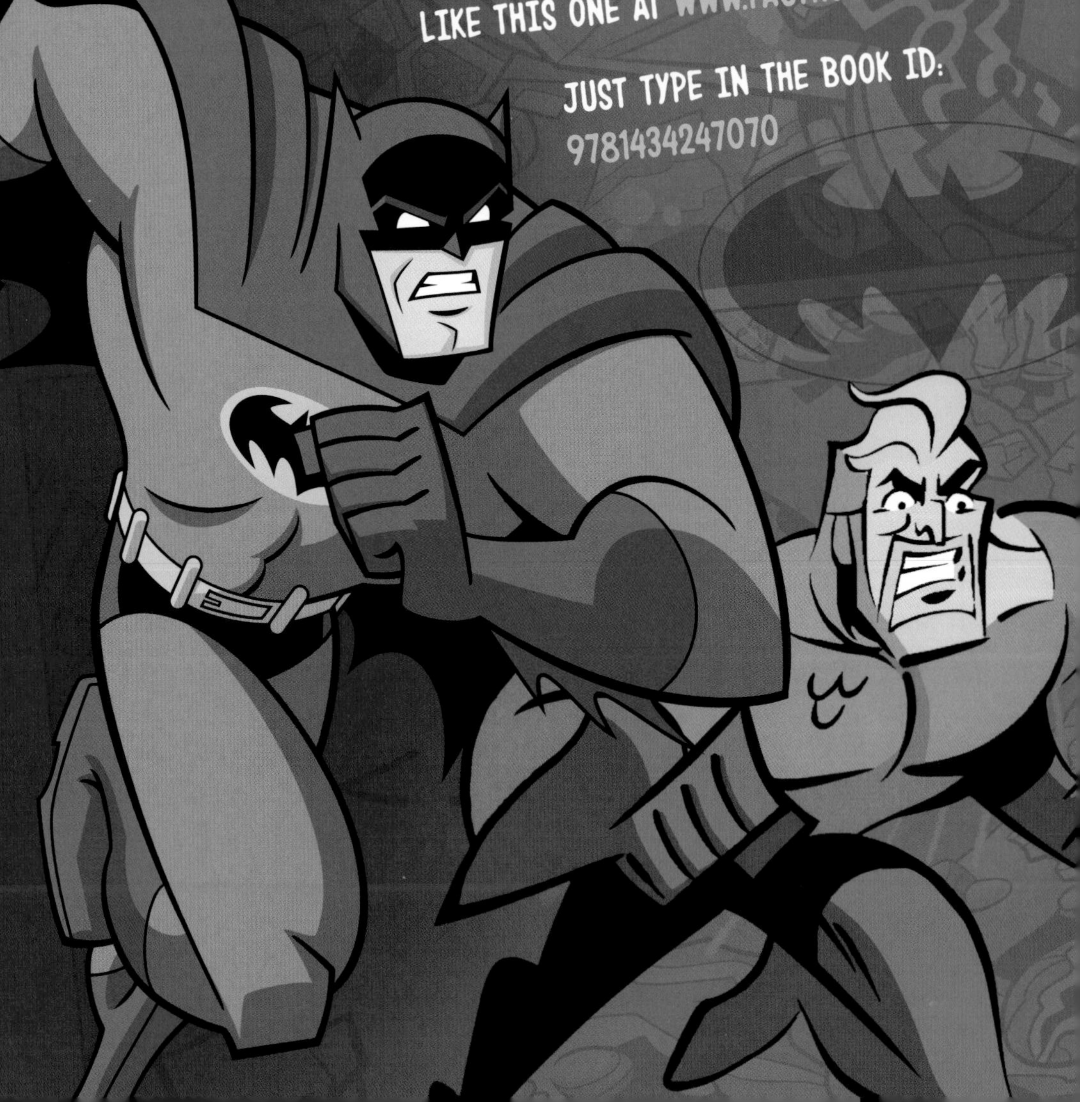